The King of
Show-and-Tell

by ABBY KLEIN

illustrated by
JOHN MCKINLEY

SCHOLASTIC INC.
New York Toronto London Auckland Sydney
Mexico City New Delhi Hong Kong Buenos Aires

To Robbie,
who, in my mind, will always be
the King of Show-and-Tell
—Mrs. K.

THE BLUE SKY PRESS

Text copyright © 2004 by Abby Klein
Illustrations copyright © 2004 by John McKinley
All rights reserved.

Special thanks to Robert Martin Staenberg.

Excerpted text on pages 79-81 is from *Are You My Mother?*
by P.D. Eastman, Random House, 1960.

ISBN-13: 978-0-439-55598-2 / ISBN-10: 0-439-55598-1
24   11 12
Printed in the United States of America 40
First Scholastic paperback printing, August 2004

CHAPTERS

I have a problem.

A really, really, big problem.

I never have anything cool

to bring for show-and-tell.

Let me tell you about it.

CHAPTER 1

An Alligator Head

"OK, everyone, come to the rug. It's time for show-and-tell," said Mrs. Wushy. "Today's sharers are Chloe and Robbie. Who would like to go first?"

"I will!" said Robbie, jumping up and running to his cubby to get his treasure.

Robbie was like the King of Show-and-Tell. The kids couldn't wait to see what he brought because he always had something really cool like a porcupine quill or a sixty-million-year-old dinosaur fossil. Today he had a real alligator head.

"This is a real alligator head," Robbie announced as oohs and ahhs filled the whole room.

"So who cares about a dumb old dead animal head?" I mumbled to myself.

"You know it's an alligator head because it has a rounded snout. Alligators have rounded snouts, and crocodiles have pointed ones."

More oohs and ahhs.

"Alligators are reptiles, so they are cold-blooded, which means they like to live in warm places. This one lived in a swamp in Florida. Questions or comments?"

When someone was done sharing, they

could pick three people in the class to ask a question or make a comment. Whenever Robbie shared, everybody's hand went up, and the kids all shouted, "Pick me! Pick me!"

"He's not going to call on anyone who's

yelling out," said Mrs. Wushy. "He's only looking for quiet people."

I turned to Jessie and whispered, "Boy, the way people are acting, you'd think they'd never seen an alligator before." I still didn't know what was so great about

it. You can see a real, live alligator at the zoo, which is way better than some stupid dead head.

"You're just jealous," she whispered back. "I think it's really cool. I wish I had an alligator head like that."

Just then Robbie called on Jessie. "I think it's really cool. Who gave it to you?"

"My mom did." Robbie looked around. "Chloe."

"My grandma has an alligator purse."

"Ha, ha, ha, she's like the song 'The Lady with the Alligator Purse,'" Max said, laughing hysterically.

"She is not," Chloe snapped. "And for your information," she continued with her hands on her hips, "that purse is very rare. My grandma has traveled all over the world, and she got that purse in Brazil. It's really special because you can't get one like it anymore."

"Yes," said Mrs. Wushy. "Many years ago, people used to make belts, shoes, and purses out of alligator skin, and they would kill the alligators just for their skin. The alligators became an endangered

species, so now it is against the law to use their skin that way. Now they're protected, and you could go to jail for selling things made from an alligator."

"Your grandma's goin' to jail," said Max.

"She is not!" cried Chloe, pointing a painted red fingernail in Max's face.

Max leaned over and bit Chloe's finger like a dog.

"Help! Help! I'm going to get rabies!" Chloe screamed, shaking her finger all around in the air.

"OK, you two. Enough!" said Mrs. Wushy. "Max, you go sit in that chair, and Chloe, you go wash off your finger. Your grandma is not going to jail. I'm sure she got it many years ago when it wasn't against the law."

"Exactly," said Chloe as she bounced off to the sink to wash her finger.

"Robbie, you get to call on one more person," said Mrs. Wushy.

I shot my arm up. Maybe if I knew where he got it, I could beg my mom to go there and get me something really cool for *my* next sharing.

"Freddy."

"Where'd your mom get it?"

"My mom got it for me last week when she went on a business trip to New York," Robbie said, shoving the alligator head in my face. "You know, she's a paleontologist. The Museum of Natural History needed her to identify some dinosaur bones while she was there. One of the scientists gave her this alligator head as a special present for me."

"New York!" I grumbled under my breath. "So much for that idea."

"Thank you, Robbie," said Mrs. Wushy, smiling. "You always bring such interesting things for show-and-tell. OK, Chloe, it's your turn. Do you need to get anything out of your cubby?"

"No, Mrs. Wushy. I have it right here in this bag," Chloe said as she sat down in front of the class and crossed her legs like some fancy lady. She pulled a package out of the bag and carefully unwrapped a pair of pink ballet slippers with satin ribbons. "These are my new ballet slippers my grandma got for me in France. They cost 300 francs and only special ballerinas get to wear them."

"Whoop-de-doo," I whispered.

"Those are lame!" Max yelled out.

"Max, that is rude," said Mrs. Wushy. "If you don't have anything nice to say, please keep your mouth shut."

"Besides," Chloe continued, "I'm not done yet. As I was saying, you can't get these in just any old store. My grandma brought them all the way from France. They have real satin ribbons, and they are the kind the prima ballerinas wear. Now I'm ready for questions or comments."

A lot of kids raised their hands. She called on Jessie first.

"Jessie."

"You are so lucky to have such a rich grandma."

"I know," Chloe said, smiling. She called on me next.

"Freddy."

"What's a franc?"

"Oh, that's what they call the money in France. I get to call on one more person. Robbie."

"Why was your grandma in France?"

"For a vacation. She has another house there. It is a really, really big castle like in a fairy tale."

"Well, thank you, Chloe," said Mrs. Wushy. "The slippers are very beautiful. Now let's see who Monday's sharers are. Freddy and Jessie, it will be your turn on Monday."

Great. I didn't have anything good to bring in. I had already shared everything from my shark collection. Nothing I ever brought in would be as cool as all the stuff Robbie and Chloe brought in. Nothing.

CHAPTER 2

For the Birds

After school, Robbie and I got on the bus. He was coming over to my house to play.

"Hey, watch where you're sitting. You almost sat on my head!"

"What are you talking about? Your head's up there, and my butt's going down here," I said, pointing to the seat.

"My alligator head. It's in that bag, and you're about to sit on it."

Ugh. That dumb head. "Sorry," I said as

I moved the bag to the side. "You know, Robbie, you're so lucky your mom brings you all those cool things when she goes to New York for her job."

"Yeah, I know."

"I wish I had something really cool to bring in for sharing."

"Hey, what do you think we should do when we get to your house?" Robbie asked, changing the subject.

"I don't know."

"Hey, let's go up to your tree house and check on the birds," Robbie said.

"What birds?" Jessie asked.

"Oh, there's this family of birds that built a nest in a branch right outside my tree house," I said. "There's a mom and three babies."

"How cute."

"Yeah, the mom always brings the babies worms to eat, and we peek out the window and watch her feed them."

"Ewww, gross. Worms are so slimy," said Chloe, wrinkling up her nose. "I would never want to be that close to something that lived in the dirt."

"They're not slimy," said Jessie. "I love

to play with them. I even ate one when I was a baby!"

"Did it crawl around in your stomach?" asked Max.

"Stop it! Stop it!" yelled Chloe with her hands over her mouth. "You ate worms! I think I'm going to be sick." She leaned over toward Max.

"Great," I thought. "Throw up right in his lap. I can't wait to see this."

"Hey, don't toss your cookies on me," said Max, squishing his body up against the window.

"You people are disgusting," said Chloe. She got up and ran to find a seat somewhere in the back of the bus.

"Good. Now I have the seat all to myself," said Max, stretching out. "Hey, guys, can I come see the birds?"

The thought of Max Sellars, the biggest bully in the whole first grade, coming to my house was enough to make *me* sick. All I could think of was that punch he had given me right in the gut once before. That was something I never wanted to experience firsthand again. I had to think fast.

"Uh, um . . . I don't think so. My mom doesn't like me to have too many kids over at a time."

"But I thought it was just going to be you and Robbie."

"Yeah, it is, but my sister has a friend coming, too."

"So?"

"So maybe some other time." *Like that will ever happen*, I thought to myself. That kid was so mean, it was bad enough he teased me all day at school. I wasn't about to invite him to my house. Besides, I could just imagine him wanting to pick up one of the birds and squeezing it to death.

Luckily, just then the bus stopped in front of my house.

"Well, gotta go. Here's my stop. Come on, Robbie."

When we got off, Robbie grabbed me by the arm. "Hey, did you mean it?"

"Mean what?"

"That you'd have Max Sellars over to your house sometime?"

"What? Are you crazy? Come on. Let's go check on the birds."

CHAPTER 3

Oh No!

Robbie and I dropped our backpacks off in my room and raced outside. We climbed up the ladder to my tree house and looked out the window.

"Oh no!" I cried.

"What?"

"The nest is empty!"

"What?" said Robbie, pushing me to the side. "How can that be? Those babies weren't old enough to fly."

"I guess they were. What a bummer. I was having fun watching them." Just then I got a sick feeling in my stomach. "You don't think the neighbor's cat got them?" I asked Robbie.

"I sure hope not. We'd better do some investigating and find out."

Robbie always wanted to do a little

investigating. He pulled his magnifying glass out of his pocket and climbed down the ladder.

"What are you looking for?" I asked as I followed him down.

"Clues."

"What kind of clues?"

"Cat and bird clues," Robbie said with his nose to the ground.

"Like what?"

"Hello . . . like maybe feathers and some bones."

"Yuck!" I said.

"Well, you didn't think the cat and the bird were going to play together, did ya?"

I was about to answer when I saw it lying there on the ground. In fact, I almost stepped on it.

"Robbie, look!"

CHAPTER 4

Look What
I Found!

"What did you find? A bone?"

"No, a baby bird," I whispered.

"What?" said Robbie, running over to where I was standing.

"Hey, be careful. Don't step on it."

"It must have fallen out of the nest."

"Do you think it's still alive?"

"I don't know," said Robbie. He bent down to get a closer look.

I got down on the ground. "Hey, listen," I said. "I think I hear it peeping."

We both lay there, holding our breath for a minute. "It *is* peeping. What do you think we should do?"

"Whatever we do," said Robbie, "we have to be really careful because it looks like it has a broken wing."

"I know. I'll go inside and get some stuff to make him a little bed," I said. "You wait here and make sure he's not lunch for the neighbor's cat."

I ran inside and raced upstairs to my room. I hit my forehead with the palm of my hand: Think, think, think. What would make a good bed? Just then I saw my baseball-card collection. I dumped out the old shoe box I was using to hold the

cards, and then I ran into the bathroom to grab an old towel to put inside.

"Freddy, is that you?" my mom called.

"Yeah, Mom, it's me. I'm just going to the bathroom."

"Do you boys want anything to eat?"

"No, thanks. We're fine," I yelled as I raced back outside.

"Is it still alive?" I asked, panting.

"Yeah, but I really think it's hurt."

"Well, I got this box and a fluffy towel to make it a soft, comfy bed."

I got down close to the baby bird and whispered, "Hey, little guy. You're going to be OK. We're going to help you. I'm just going to put you in this nice, warm box." As I reached to pick him up, his peeping got louder. "I think he's crying. His wing must really hurt."

We put him in the box and carried it up
the ladder to the tree house. "What now?"
I asked Robbie.

"We need to put some holes in the top
of the box, so he can breathe."

Robbie poked some holes in the top of
the box with a pencil.

"Great! Now what?"

"Maybe we should go get him some-thing to eat."

"Good idea," I said. "Like what?"

"What's in your fridge?" asked Robbie.

"Pizza, leftover meatloaf, string cheese."

"How about the pizza?" Robbie said.

"Really? I didn't know birds ate pizza."

"They don't, Ding-Dong," said Robbie, laughing. "I'm just kidding."

"Well, what then?"

"I bet he'd like some nice, juicy worms."

"Worms, yeah. Good idea," I said.

I stuck my head down near the box and whispered, "You stay here, little guy. We'll

be right back. We're just going to get you some lunch."

I heard a little "peep."

"You're welcome," I said.

Robbie and I grabbed our bug-collector jar and tweezers and climbed down the ladder. We went to the back of the yard where there was some gloppy, gooey mud. It was our favorite place to look for creepy crawlers.

"Ooh, look at this roly-poly. He's *huge*," I said, picking it up and rolling it around in my hand. "Maybe the little bird would like this. It looks really juicy."

"Nah," said Robbie. "Worms are better. But check out this trail of ants. They all look like they're carrying a cookie crumb into their hole. Maybe if they put them all

together down there, they'll have one giant cookie."

"That'd be pretty funny."

We dug around some more. "What if we can't find any worms?" I asked.

"Well, it's not exactly the best time of day to be hunting worms," Robbie said.

"What do you mean?"

"Haven't you ever heard someone say, 'The early bird catches the worm'?"

"No."

"Well, the best time to catch a worm is early in the morning, so the birds that get up first get the most worms."

"Good thing I'm not a bird, because I hate getting up in the morning." I stuck my fingers deeper into the mud. "Oh, wait! I think I found one!"

"Let me see." Robbie leaned over and stuck his face so close to the ground he got mud on his nose.

"Move over. I can't see through your big head," I said, pushing him out of the way. I grabbed my tweezers and yanked the fat, wriggling worm out of the mud. "Don't you look delicious," I said, dangling the worm between my fingers. I dropped it into my bug jar and searched around for some more.

By the time we were done, Robbie and I had found six delicious worms for the little bird. We carried them back up the ladder to the tree house.

"I think now we should give him a name," I said.

"Yeah, how 'bout the name Josh?" Robbie suggested.

"No, no, no. Not a people name. He needs a bird name."

"How 'bout Feathers?"

"No. I think I'll call him Winger."

"Winger? What kind of name is that? And how come you get to choose?" asked Robbie.

"I found him, didn't I?"

"So?"

"So that means I get to pick his name, and he looks like a Winger to me."

I carefully picked up the little bird and kissed his tiny head. "Are you hungry, little Winger?"

"Peep."

"See! He answered me. He said yes."

"No, he said, 'Peep.' That's what birds do. They peep."

"How 'bout a fat, juicy worm?" I said to Winger, ignoring Robbie. "Don't worry, little guy. I speak Bird, and I'll take good care of you. I promise," I said as I gently fed him one of the worms.

CHAPTER 5

Night Rescue

I had left Winger safely in his box in the tree house because I didn't want my mom to see him. Being The Neat Freak that she was, she *really* didn't like it when I brought animals into the house. Once I brought a frog home, and she screamed her head off. She told me *never* to bring anything like that into the house *ever* again.

But now I couldn't stop thinking of him as I lay in bed. It was dark. He was all alone up there. No mommy to take care of him. He was probably crying, "Peep, peep."

I sat up in bed. Oh no! The neighbor's cat! He likes to go out at night. I had to go rescue Winger before it was too late.

I waited until the house was quiet. Until everyone was asleep. Then I grabbed my special sharkhead flashlight and tiptoed down the stairs, making sure I skipped the one that squeaks. The lock on the back door was really hard to turn.

"Oh, come on, come on," I whispered. "Just open."

The lock finally clicked, and I opened the door really slowly so it wouldn't creak.

I stepped out into the yard, and the chilly night air made me shiver. The cold, wet grass turned my bare feet to ice, but I kept walking toward the tree house. "I'm

coming, Winger," I whispered. "Don't be scared. I'll save you."

I climbed the rungs of the ladder very slowly because it was hard to see in the dark. Just as I reached the top, I heard a little "peep."

I sighed a big sigh and ran over to pick the little bird up. "It's OK. I'm here now. You don't need to be scared anymore," I whispered into his little head. "You can come sleep with me tonight. I'll take you to my room where it's warm and cozy."

I put Winger back in his box and closed the top, so he wouldn't fall out as I climbed back down the ladder.

Climbing back down was a little tricky in the dark, holding both my flashlight and the box, but I managed to make it down without dropping Winger.

I was walking back across the grass when all of a sudden I saw my dad running toward me with a baseball bat. He was yelling, "WHO'S OUT HERE? I'LL CALL THE POLICE!"

I froze. At first I couldn't say anything.
Then I started screaming, "DAD, DAD . . .
IT'S ME . . . IT'S FREDDY!"

"Freddy? What are you doing out here
in the middle of the night? I thought you
were a robber."

"I was um . . ." I stammered. "I was just
getting my baseball cards," I said, showing
him the box. "Robbie and I were trading
cards out here today, and I left the box in

the tree house by accident. I didn't want them to be out here all night."

"Well, you scared me half to death!" my dad shouted. "I don't ever want you to sneak around like that in the middle of the night! It's really unsafe."

"OK, sure, Dad," I said, pretending to yawn. "I'm just going to go back to bed." I didn't want to keep talking. My feet were

freezing, and I was sure Winger was going to peep any minute.

"Come on. I'll tuck you back in."

When we got upstairs, I put the box down on the floor next to my bed.

"Good night, Dad."

"Good night," he said and started to walk out of the room.

"Peep."

He turned back. "Did you just say something?"

"Huh?"

"I thought I heard you say something."

"Nope. I was just yawning, Dad," I said, faking another yawn.

"Well, good night."

I waited for his footsteps to disappear down the hall, then I turned on my lamp and opened the top of the box. "Sorry. Are you all right?"

"Peep," Winger answered.

"Would you like to come up here and sleep with me?"

"Peep, peep."

I picked up the box and put it right next to my pillow.

"Good night, Winger. Sleep tight."

"Peep."

CHAPTER 6

Shhh...
Don't Tell

"Hey, Birdbrain, you're going to miss *Commander Upchuck* if you don't hurry up," Suzie called as she walked toward my bed. It was Saturday morning, and Suzie and I usually watched cartoons until our mom and dad got up.

"Huh?" I said, half asleep, yawning and rubbing my eyes.

"You're going to . . ." Suzie stopped. Now she was standing right next to the bed. "What is *that*?" she asked, pointing to my pillow.

"What?"

"That."

I rolled over to see where she was pointing. All of a sudden my eyes snapped open. Oh my gosh—Winger. I had forgotten all about him. But it was too late. I couldn't hide him now. She had seen him. "A baby bird," I whispered.

"You are in *sooo* much trouble. Just wait till Mom sees this. She is really going to freak out. You know how much she hates animals in the house."

"Please don't tell her," I begged. "I'll do anything."

"Anything?"

"Yeah. Anything."

"OK. I'll make you a deal. I will keep your little secret if you make my bed for a whole entire week."

"A *week*?"

"You said anything. Now do we have a deal or not?"

"Deal," I said as we locked pinkies.

"And I get your dessert at lunch every day for a week."

"What?! You can't do that! We already pinkied it."

"Fine, then. Deal's off."

"Oh, all right. Deal," I said as we locked pinkies one more time.

I reached down and lifted Winger out of the box. "I found him yesterday. He fell out of his nest. His mom is gone, and I think his wing is broken. He needs me."

"He is sorta cute."

"Peep."

"Do you want to hold him?"

"I don't want to hurt him."

"It's OK," I said as I gently handed him to Suzie.

"Peep."

"See? He likes you."

"Hey, little guy."

"Peep."

"He must be starving."

"I gave him some worms yesterday."

"Ewww."

"Well, *he* loved 'em."

"How 'bout something to drink?"

"Huh?"

"He has to drink, you know."

"I don't have a bottle of milk."

"Baby birds don't drink milk. They're not mammals. They drink water."

"Oh."

"And they don't drink from bottles."

"So how *do* they drink?"

"They lick water off the mom's beak."

"I don't have a beak."

"Well don't look at *me*! I'm not letting some bird lick my mouth."

"What should we do?"

"You know, one time on this nature show, I saw a guy give a baby bird some water with a medicine dropper."

"Yeah."

"I'll go and check the medicine cabinet," Suzie said.

Suzie ran out and came back with the medicine dropper and a cup of water. "OK. You hold him while I try to put the drops in his mouth."

I held Winger in my hands, and Suzie squeezed the dropper. The first few drops fell into Winger's eye.

"Sorry, little guy, but you've got to open your mouth like this," I said as I opened my mouth real wide.

"Peep."

"Now you try it."

When Suzie squeezed the dropper again, he opened his mouth and swallowed the water. "Now you got the hang of it."

"Remember, you can't say anything about this to Mom and Dad," I said.

"As long as you keep up your end of the deal, I'll keep up mine."

"You know, you're the best sister in the whole world."

"I know."

CHAPTER 7

Peep

I was able to keep Winger a secret all week-end. But now it was Monday morning, and I had to find a way to get him to school.

Today *I* was going to be the King of Show-and-Tell. *I* was going to have something better than Robbie. Something that all the kids would think was really cool.

I just had to figure out how to get Winger to school today without my mom finding out.

I carefully put Winger in his box and

ran downstairs for breakfast with the box hidden under my arm.

"Oh, there you are," said my mom. "I thought you had fallen back asleep. You have to start getting up earlier. You know, there's an old saying that the early bird catches the worm."

"Yeah," I said and laughed. "Robbie told me that once."

"Well, what would you like to eat for breakfast?"

"Peep."

"What was that?"

"What was what?"

"Peep."

"That. It sounded like your box just said 'peep.'"

"Mom, I think you're going crazy. Boxes don't peep."

"Well, I could've sworn I heard a bird chirping."

"You did," Suzie said.

I glared at her and mouthed the words, "I thought we had a deal."

"You heard that little blue jay that's right outside the window."

"Thank you," I mouthed back.

"Well, it sure sounded like it was right here in this room," my mom said.

"Honey, there aren't any birds in the kitchen," my dad said from behind his newspaper.

"Anyway, Freddy, why do you have your baseball-card box with you?"

I hadn't thought that far ahead yet, so I said, "Mom, can I have some of that Sugar Cookie Crunch?"

"Sure, honey," she said, pouring me a bowl of cereal. "Here you go."

"Peep."

"There it is again," my mom said. "You must have heard that."

My dad put down his paper. "Honey, why don't you go back to bed? I think you're still a little tired."

"I know you all think I'm crazy, but there is something peeping in this kitchen!"

"Maybe it's the fire alarm," Suzie said.

"Yeah," I said. "Whenever the battery is low, they make that bird-peeping sound."

"Good thinking, kids," said my dad. Then he turned to my mom. "I'm sure that's what it is, honey. I'll check when I'm done with breakfast."

"OK." She turned back to me. "Freddy,

you still haven't answered my question. Why do you have your baseball-card box with you?"

"Ummm . . . because I have to bring it to school." Boy, was that a dumb answer.

"You do? I thought you weren't allowed to bring trading cards to school."

"You're not, but . . ." I turned to Suzie and mouthed, "Help me!"

"Yeah, normally you're not," she butted in, "but today is a special day in first grade, and you can bring them in just for today."

"Yeah, just for today Mrs. Wushy said you could share your special collections."

"Really? Well then why aren't you bringing in your shark collection?" my mom asked.

"Because the kids have already seen all of my shark stuff, but they haven't seen my baseball cards."

"Well, OK, if Mrs. Wushy said it was all right," said my mom. "I just don't want you to lose them."

"Oh, I won't," I said, hugging the box close. "I won't."

CHAPTER 8

The King of Show-and-Tell

I didn't want the kids to see Winger until it was time for show-and-tell. I wanted it to be a big surprise. If I brought him in the box, the kids would start asking me questions as soon as I got in the door. "Is that your show-and-tell?" "What's in the box?" "Can I look in the box?" No. I would have to hide him until show-and-tell time.

Before the bell rang, I hid behind the playhouse and carefully lifted him out of the box and put him in the pocket of my sweatshirt jacket.

"Peep."

"It's OK, Winger," I whispered into the pocket. "You'll be all right in there."

Brrrinnnggg. Brrrinnggg. Brrringgg. The bell was ringing. It was time to go in.

"Peep."

"Shhh. We don't want anyone to hear you. Now go to sleep," I said.

I left the box behind the playhouse and walked into the classroom.

"Hey," Robbie said, grabbing my arm. "How's that little bird we found?"

"Oh, he's fine."

"Is his wing getting better?"

"Yeah, I think it's almost all better."

"Maybe I can come see him today."

"Oh, you'll see him today." I smiled as I went to sit down on the rug.

"Good morning, everyone," said Mrs. Wushy. "This morning I am going to read you one of my favorite stories, *Are You My Mother?* It's about a little bird who falls out of a tree and goes looking for his mother."

"I think you're going to like this one, Winger," I whispered into my pocket.

"Did you say something, Freddy?" asked Mrs. Wushy.

"Oh, um . . . I was just telling Robbie that I think I'm going to like this one."

"Yes, but now I need you to zip your lips and be a good listener."

Mrs. Wushy started to read. As she read,

I put my hand in my pocket and rubbed Winger's head, hoping that it would keep him quiet. "'"Are you my mother?" he said to the kitten.'"

"Peep."

"' "Are you my mother?" he said to the hen.'"

"Peep."

Mrs. Wushy stopped. "Boys and girls, whoever is making that peeping sound needs to stop. I don't think it's funny."

She continued, "'"Are you my mother?" he said to the dog.'"

"Peep."

"Max, is that you?" asked Mrs. Wushy.

"No," said Max, laughing.

"I told you I didn't like it when you made noises while I was trying to read."

"It's not me."

She continued, "'"Are you my mother?" he said to the cow.'"

"Peep."

"Max, that is enough. You are being rude and interrupting the class. Please go sit in a chair."

"B-b-but," Max stammered.

"No buts. Go sit in that chair. You are in time-out," said Mrs. Wushy.

I really did not like Max Sellars. He was always so mean to everyone. He was the biggest bully in the whole first grade, so I shouldn't really care that he was getting a time-out for something he didn't do. He deserved it for all the other times he had

done stuff to us and had never gotten caught. But I couldn't help myself. I still felt bad for him. He was getting in trouble for something that I did.

"It's not Max."

"Excuse me?" said Mrs. Wushy.

"It's not Max," I said. "He didn't do it."

"Well then, who did?"

"I did."

"You did?" asked Mrs. Wushy.

"Well, not me, exactly."

"What are you talking about?" Mrs. Wushy asked, exasperated.

"Actually, it was a bird," I said.

"Freddy, there are no birds in our classroom, and if you don't explain this to me in one minute, you are going to be in time-out, too!"

I pulled Winger out of my pocket.

"Oh, he's so cute," said Jessie.

"Ewww, he's all dirty, and he's covered with germs. Get him away from me!" said Chloe, jumping to her feet.

"Freddy," said Mrs. Wushy, "why do you have a bird in your pocket?"

"Please don't be mad, Mrs. Wushy," I said, beginning to sniffle. "I just wanted to bring something real cool for show-and-tell, and I wanted it to be a surprise."

"Well, that certainly is a surprise."

"Can we hold it? Can we hold it?" all the kids started asking.

"Freddy, I should be angry that you sneaked this bird into class and interrupted the story."

"Sorry." I sniffled harder as a tear rolled down my cheek.

"But I'm not."

"You're not?"

"No, I'm actually proud of you that you stood up for Max. You were a good friend, and you told the truth because you didn't want him to get a time-out for something he didn't do."

"Max," said Mrs. Wushy, "I think I owe you an apology. I'm very sorry. I should have believed you when you told me it wasn't you making that sound."

"Can I come back to the rug now, Mrs. Wushy?" Max asked. "I want to see Freddy's cool bird."

"Of course you can, Max. Freddy, would you like to come up and share your bird with the class?"

As I walked to the front of the room, I could hear the kids' oohs and aahs, and the chorus of "Let me see! I want to see!" I went to sit down on the sharing chair, but today it wasn't just any old chair. It was a throne. Because today I was the King of Show-and-Tell.

DEAR READER,

I have been a teacher for many years, and every day in my class we have show-and-tell. My students love to bring in special things from home to share with the rest of the class.

One time a little boy brought in a real alligator head just like Robbie's. Another time a little girl brought a tarantula to share, and she put it on my head. Boy, was I scared!

I hope you have as much fun reading *The King of Show-and-Tell* as I had writing it.

HAPPY READING!

Freddy's Fun Pages

FREDDY'S SHARK JOURNAL

BABY SHARKS

Baby sharks are called pups. Some baby sharks hatch from eggs, just like baby birds!

The mommy shark lays the eggs in the water. The eggs stay in an egg case that is hard and protects the baby shark until it hatches into the ocean.

Other sharks grow from eggs inside their mom's body and are born alive into the ocean.

When the baby shark is born, the mommy shark doesn't take care of it. It has to take care of itself—just like Winger before I rescued him. My mom does so much for me. I'm glad I'm not a shark!

SUZIE'S SECRET RIDDLE

Use the code below to find the answer to my riddle.
—Suzie

a	b	d	e	f	h	i	k
☺	★	□	✳	%	▲	✓	+

l	o	r	s	t	u	y
♥	#	@	→	$	●	⊠

What do you get when you cross a parrot and a shark?

A b i f d · T H A T
☺ ★ ✓ @ □ · $ ▲ ☺ $

T A l K S · y o u r
$ ☺ ♥ + → · ⊠ # ● @

e a r O f f !
✳ ☺ @ · # % %

90

A VERY SILLY STORY
by Freddy Thresher

Help Freddy write a silly story by filling in the blanks
on the next three pages. The description under each
blank tells you what kind of word to use. Don't read
the story until you have filled in all the blanks!

HELPFUL HINTS:

A **verb** is an action word (such as run, jump, or hide).
An **adjective** describes a person, place, or thing
(such as smelly, loud, or blue).

One day after school, _____ and I were

a friend

_____ for a _____ _____

a verb ending in -ing   an adjective   an insect

in my backyard. As we _____ under

a verb ending in -ed

the _____, we heard a _____

a place outside   an adjective

sound. It was coming from a pile of _____

an adjective

_____ on the ground.

things

"Look!" I said. "It's a baby_____!"

an animal

We picked up the baby_____ , and we

the same animal

_____ him inside my _____.

a verb ending in -ed   something you wear

"We need to _____ this _____

a verb   an adjective

guy some _____!" I said.

a type of food

Then, _____ carefully carried

the same friend

the baby _____ up to my room while

the same animal

I went to the _____ .

another room in your house

"Can I get some _____?" I asked

a type of food

_____ .

a family member

"Can't you wait until we _____

a verb

dinner?"_____ said.

the same family member

"Well," I said, thinking fast, "we have to draw

pictures of _____ for our homework

                the same type of food

assignment. Can you give me a few pieces of

_____ , a _____ ,

    a crunchy food   *a soft food*

and some_____?"

        a drink

I put everything in a _____ _____

        an adjective   *a thing*

and ran upstairs. We had put the baby_____

        the same animal

in an empty _____ with a_____

    something in your room   *an adjective*

_____ for a bed. The baby_____ ate

  a thing   *the same animal*

a little of the _____ and all of the

      the same crunchy food

_____ , but he hated the _____ .

  the same drink   *the same soft food*

"What shall we _____ him?" I asked.

        a verb

"Let's _____ him _____ ,

    the same verb   *the same drink*

since that's his favorite," said _____ .

        the same friend

FREDDY'S WINTER BIRD FEEDER

It's hard for birds like Winger to find food in the winter. Just follow these simple steps, and you can make a neat bird feeder for the birds outside your home!
—Freddy

1. Find a large pinecone.

2. Tie a piece of string to the top of the pinecone.

3. Cover the pinecone with peanut butter.

4. Roll the pinecone in birdseed.

5. Hang your bird feeder from a tree branch in your yard or outside a window, and watch the birds gobble up the seeds.

MAZE

See if you can find the way
to Winger's nest.

nest

Start here

Freddy has *another* problem— a really, really, big problem!

FREDDY THRESHER is the *only* one in his class who hasn't lost a tooth. Now, Max the bully is calling him a baby, and Freddy's ready to do anything to get one of those pesky teeth to fall out.

Read all about it in *Tooth Trouble*!

And don't miss Freddy's hilarious adventures in *Homework Hassles*. . . .

Freddy has to write a report on a nocturnal animal. So why not stay up all night and do some outdoor research with his best friend, Robbie? Freddy's ready for some midnight fun, but nothing turns out the way it's planned!